My
Robot

My Robot

Eve Bunting

Illustrated by Dagmar Fehlau

Green Light Readers
Harcourt, Inc.

Orlando   Austin   New York   San Diego   Toronto   London

I got a new robot for my birthday.
I call him Cecil.

Ever since I got him, we have been
doing lots of things together.

Cecil plays tag with the children at school.
Whir! Whir! We hear the sound of his wheels
spinning as he races after us. Sometimes he
goes a little too fast.

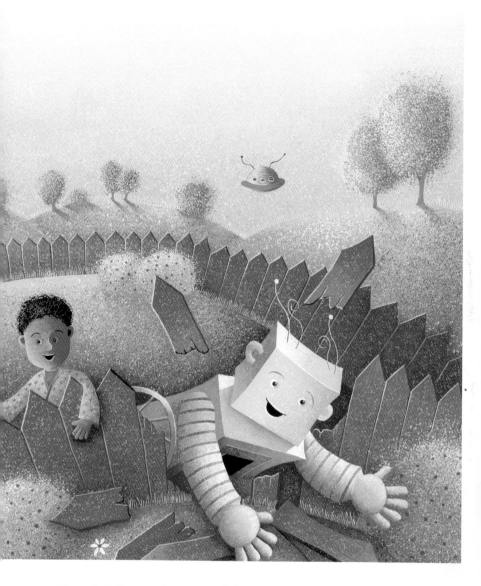

Crash! Smash! Cecil hits the fence.
"Not the fence, Cecil!" I call. It's hard
not to laugh. Playing tag is not the
best thing my robot can do.

All my friends at school like Cecil a lot. He helps our teacher, Mr. Spencer. Helping Mr. Spencer is not the best thing my robot can do.

Cecil leads the school band.
Rum-a-tum-tum. Hear that drum.
"Don't dance, Cecil!" I say. "Don't prance! Just
march!" Leading the band is not the best thing
any robot can do.

Cecil picks me up after school.
He gives me a ride home.
"How's the weather up there?"my little brother
Dennis asks. He gets a ride home, too.

nce in a while, Cecil does tricks with our dog,
rince. They can roll over. *Whirl! Whirl!*
hey can beg. *Creak! Fizz! Whiz!*
hake, Prince," says Dennis. "Shake, Cecil!"
oing tricks is not the best thing my robot
an do.

Cecil plays hide-and-seek, too. He is always
IT. He gives everyone a chance to find a good
place to hide.

Clank! Clunk! Here comes Cecil!
We don't say we heard him coming. He whistles
when he finds us. *Whir! Spark! Pop!* Playing
hide-and-seek is not the best thing my robot
can do.

Everyone has heard about Cecil's cakes.
He makes circus animals with the frosting.
His cakes are almost too pretty to eat.
"This is your best cake yet!" says Dennis.

"Cecil's cakes are pretty good," I say, "but that
is still not the best thing my robot can do."
"My tummy tells me it is," Dennis says.

Cecil can mow the grass. *Whir! Wheeze! Whish!*
Cecil goes very fast. It's a hot day, but Dad is
not hot.

"This MUST be the best thing Cecil can do,"
says Dad.
"Almost," I tell Dad. "You and Dennis come
with me. I'll show you something else Cecil
can do."

"Look in here. Even cleaning my room
is not the best thing my robot can do."
I give Cecil a hug.

"Thanks, Cecil," I whisper. "The very best thing you can do is be my friend!"
Flash! Spark! Whirl! Pop!
Cecil knows.

Ready Robot Puppets

If you had a robot, how would your robot help you? Make a robot puppet and act out all the ways it could help.

WHAT YOU'LL NEED

 a cardboard tube or rolled-up paper

 collage materials

 tape

 construction paper

 glue

 markers or crayons

. Use the tube for the robot's body.
raw a face on the tube.

2. Add arms and legs
to the robot's body.

. Decorate your robot.
hink of things you would
e your robot to do for you.

e your creation to show how
obot could help you.

Meet the Author and Illustrator

Eve Bunting once met a robot. Students had made him out of cardboard. He was a great robot! She thought about how grand it would be to have her very own robot. Then she decided to write this story about it! She is very happy to share *My Robot* with you.

Eve Bunting

Dagmar Fehlau was born in Germany, and then came to the United States to study art. She always loved drawing and painting, so she knew she would be an artist when she grew up. She hopes you like the pictures in *My Robot*.

Dagmar Fehla

www.HarcourtBooks.com

First Green Light Readers edition 2006

Green Light Readers is a trademark of Harcourt, Inc., registered in the
United States of America and/or other jurisdictions.

Library of Congress Cataloging-in-Publication Data
Bunting, Eve, 1928–
My robot/by Eve Bunting; illustrated by Dagmar Fehlau.
p. cm.
"Green Light Readers."
Summary: Cecil the robot is good at playing tag, leading the school band, and
performing tricks with the dog, but there is one important thing he does best of all.
[1. Automata—Fiction. 2. Friendship—Fiction.]
I. Fehlau, Dagmar, ill. II. Title. III. Series.
PZ7.B91527Myr 2006
[E]—dc22   2005006936
ISBN-13: 978-0152-05593-6 ISBN-10: 0-15-205593-2
ISBN-13: 978-0152-05617-9 (pb) ISBN-10: 0-15-205617-3 (pb)

C E G H F D B
C E G H F D B (pb)

Ages 5–7
Grades: 1
Guided Reading Level: G–H
Reading Recovery Level: 12–13

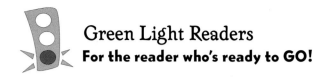

Green Light Readers
For the reader who's ready to GO!

"A must-have for any family with a beginning reader."—*Boston Sunday Herald*

"You can't go wrong with adding several copies of these terrific books to your beginning-to-read collection."—*School Library Journal*

"A winner for the beginner."—*Booklist*

Five Tips to Help Your Child Become a Great Reader

1. Get involved. Reading aloud to and with your child is just as important as encouraging your child to read independently.

2. Be curious. Ask questions about what your child is reading.

3. Make reading fun. Allow your child to pick books on subjects that interest her or him.

4. Words are everywhere—not just in books. Practice reading signs, packages, and cereal boxes with your child.

5. Set a good example. Make sure your child sees YOU reading.

Why Green Light Readers Is the Best Series for Your New Reader

● Created exclusively for beginning readers by some of the biggest and brightest names in children's books

● Reinforces the reading skills your child is learning in school

● Encourages children to read—and finish—books by themselves

● Offers extra enrichment through fun, age-appropriate activities unique to each story

● Incorporates characteristics of the Reading Recovery program used by educators

● Developed with Harcourt School Publishers and credentialed educational consultants